The Gol

Guardian Of The Deep

Neel Lak

Copyright and Publishing Rights -   Neel

ISBN: 9798346192220
Imprint: Independently published

Contents

Chapter 1:

The Fishing Village

The salty breeze ruffled Felix's unruly dark hair as he raced down the worn wooden dock, his bare feet pattering against the sun-bleached planks. "Felix! Wait up!" called his twelve-year-old sister, Joanna, her long brown braid swinging as she hurried after him. Felix skidded to a stop at the edge of the dock, his eyes shining excitedly as he watched the fishing boats bob gently in the harbour.

The village of Coral Cove was coming to life around them with the murmur of voices and the creaking of vessels as they were unloaded."Do you think Dad caught a lot of fish last night?" Felix asked, bouncing on his toes as he scanned the horizon for their father's boat, the Sea Whisper. Joanna shaded her eyes with her hand, squinting against the rising sun. "I hope so. Mom said the catches have been smaller lately."

As if summoned by their conversation, the Sea Whisper appeared around the headland, its white sail billowing in the morning breeze. Felix let out a whoop of excitement, waving his arms wildly."There he is! Come on, Jo! Let's help him unload!"The siblings raced to the end of the dock where their father, Marcus, was expertly guiding the boat alongside. His weathered face broke into a warm smile as he saw his children."Ahoy there, my little sea urchins!" he called, tossing them a rope. "Mind giving your old man a hand?"Felix caught the rope with practised ease, quickly securing it to the dock. Joanna was already reaching for the fish baskets, her nose wrinkling slightly at the pungent smell. As they worked together to unload the catch, Felix couldn't help but notice that the baskets seemed lighter than usual.

He glanced at his father, seeing the slight furrow in his brow that usually meant worry."Dad," Felix started hesitantly, "is everything okay? There doesn't seem to be as many fish as before."Marcus paused, running a hand through his salt-and-pepper hair. "You've got keen eyes, son. The sea's been changing lately. Fish that used to be plentiful are getting harder to find."Joanna looked up from the basket she was carrying. "Is it because of the big ships we sometimes see on the horizon? I heard Mrs. Guthrie at the market say they're taking all our fish."

Their father shook his head. "It's not that simple, Jo. Something is going on out there we don't quite understand yet."As they finished unloading, the tantalising smell of freshly baked bread wafted down from their cottage on the hill. Their mother, Anna, appeared at the top of the path, waving to them."Breakfast's ready!" she called. "Come on up before it gets cold!"

As they climbed the path home, Felix's mind was filled with questions. What was happening to the fish? Why was the sea changing? He was so lost in thought that he almost missed the old fisherman, Gramps Pete, calling out to them."Ahoy there, young'uns!" the old man's voice creaked like old timber.

Has your pa told you the tale of the Golden Guardian yet?"Felix and Joanna exchanged excited glances. They loved Gramps Pete's stories."No, we haven't heard that one," Joanna said eagerly. Gramps Pete's eyes twinkled mischievously. "Well then, you come by my cottage this evening, and I'll spin you a yarn that'll make your eyes pop! It's a tale of magic and mystery, of a fish with scales of pure gold that guards the secrets of the sea."As they continued up the path, Felix could hardly contain his excitement. A golden fish? Could it be real? And if it was, could it have something to do with the changes in the sea? Little did Felix know, but this was the beginning of an adventure that would change their lives forever. As they stepped into their cottage, the aroma of breakfast filled the air.

Chapter 2

Strange Tides

The sun was setting over Coral Cove. The sky looked like a painting with brilliant oranges and pinks. Felix sat on the weathered steps of Gramps Pete's cottage, his legs swinging impatiently. Joanna sat beside him, braiding a piece of seagrass."Do you think the Golden Guardian is real?" Felix asked excitedly. Joanna shrugged, but her eyes sparkled with curiosity. "I don't know. Gramps Pete's stories are usually just tall tales."Before Felix could respond, the cottage door creaked open. Gramps Pete emerged, his white beard glowing in the fading light.

"Ah, there you are", he said, lowering himself onto a rickety chair. " Are you ready for a tale of mystery and magic?"The children nodded eagerly coming closer. Gramps's voice dropped to a dramatic whisper. "They say that long ago when the sea was young, a fish with scales of pure gold swam these waters. It wasn't just any fish, mind you. This was the Guardian of the Sea, protector of all ocean life."Felix's eyes widened. "What happened to it?""Some say it still swims in the deepest parts of the ocean," Gramps Pete continued.

Others say it vanished when humans started taking too much from the sea. But I'll tell you a secret." He leaned in close. "On nights when the moon is full and the tide is high, if you listen carefully, you might hear its song on the wind."Felix couldn't stop thinking about the Golden Guardian on the way home. Could it be real? And if it was, could it help with their father's and villagers' problems? The next morning, Felix and Joanna joined their parents at the dock. The mood was sombre as they helped unload the day's catch."Another small haul," their father sighed, lifting a half-empty basket. Their mother, Anna, placed a comforting hand on his shoulder. "We'll make do, Marcus. We always have.

"We'll make do, Marcus. We always have."As the children carried baskets to the market, they overheard snippets of worried conversations."...never seen the fishing this bad...""...something strange in the water...""...what if we can't make a living anymore?" That night at dinner, the usual cheerful chatter was replaced by tense silence. Felix pushed his food around his plate, his mind racing.

"Mom, Dad," he said suddenly. "What if there's something wrong with the sea itself?"His parents exchanged a look."What do you mean, Felix?" his father asked."Well," Felix hesitated, glancing at Joanna for support. "We've heard people talking— about strange things in the water. And the fish are disappearing. What if it's all connected?"Their mother sighed. "We don't know, sweetheart. The sea has always had its mysteries."Later that night, Felix heard a soft knock at his door as he lay in bed. Joanna slipped in, her face pale in the moonlight.

"Felix," she whispered. "I can't sleep. I keep thinking about what you said at dinner. What if there is something wrong with the sea?"Felix sat up, a plan already forming in his mind. "Then we need to find out what it is."Joanna's eyes widened.

"What are you suggesting?"Tonight's a full moon," Felix said, a mischievous glint in his eye. "Remember what Gramps Pete said about the Guardian's song? Maybe we could..."Joanna bit her lip, torn between curiosity and caution. "But we're not supposed to go out at night.""I know," Felix admitted. "But this is important. Don't you want to help Dad and the village?"After a moment's hesitation, Joanna nodded. "Okay. But not tonight. We should plan this properly.""Tomorrow night then," Felix whispered. "The moon will still be full, and we can figure out the best time to sneak out."Joanna stood to leave, pausing at the door. "Felix? What if we find something?""Then maybe we can save the village," Felix replied, but his voice held a hint of uncertainty. As Joanna slipped back to her room, neither child could have guessed what awaited them the following night, when they would discover just how mysterious their beloved sea had become.

Chapter 3

Midnight Discovery

Felix couldn't sleep. Gramps Pete's words about the full moon kept echoing in his mind. He tossed and turned until a pebble pinged against his window. Joanna stood in the yard below, her dark hair glowing silver in the moonlight." I knew you'd be awake," she whispered when he joined her outside. "Come on, I can't wait for tomorrow. Let's go tonight ". They crept through the sleeping village, past the idle fishing boats that creaked softly in the harbour. The full moon hung low over the water, painting a shimmering path across the waves. The tide was unusually high, just as Gramps Pete had mentioned.

"We shouldn't be out here," Joanna said, but her voice held more excitement than concern. They made their way along the shoreline, avoiding the sharp rocks that dotted the beach. Felix stopped suddenly. "Look at this." He pointed to a dark patch on the sand that gleamed oddly in the moonlight. Joanna crouched down, running her finger through it."Oil," she said, wiping her hand on a nearby rock. "And there's more over there."

She was right – small black puddles dotted the beach like inkblots. As they walked further, they found tidepools that usually teemed with life strangely quiet. A hermit crab stumbled sideways, its movements jerky and unnatural. Nearby, a starfish looked pale and sickly, its usually vibrant colours dulled to a ghostly white."Something's wrong," Felix whispered. "The sea is sick."A cool breeze carried the tang of salt and something else – a metallic smell that made them wrinkle their noses. The waves seemed to whisper secrets in a language just beyond their understanding. Joanna grabbed Felix's arm. "Did you see that?"At first, Felix saw nothing but moonlight on the water. Then a golden glimmer caught his eye, beneath the waves. It was faint, like sunshine trapped underwater, moving with a purpose."The Golden Guardian?" Felix breathed, hardly daring to hope. The glow grew stronger, creating patterns in the water that couldn't be explained by moonlight alone. It moved parallel to the shore, following the curve of the bay.

Joanna took a step closer to the water's edge. "It's beautiful.

"Suddenly, the light vanished. The water went dark, but the darkness was different now – deeper, as if something massive was displacing the water beneath the surface. A gentle swell rolled toward them, lifting the water several feet higher than the surrounding waves. Felix and Joanna stumbled backwards as the swell reached the shore. The water drew back, leaving fresh oil stains on the sand. In the distance, something broke the surface – just for a moment – something much larger than any fish they'd ever seen."We need to tell someone," Joanna said, her voice trembling with fear and awe."Who would believe us?" Felix asked, his eyes still fixed on the water where the creature had disappeared. "We need proof first."They stood there for a long moment, the midnight breeze carrying the sounds of the troubled sea. Whatever they had seen tonight, they knew their lives would never be quite the same.

Chapter 4

The Golden Fish

The massive shape beneath the waves moved closer to shore, and Felix and Joanna backed away from the water's edge. Then they heard a sound so faint, that it might have been their imagination. A whimper, like a wounded animal."Listen," Joanna whispered, grabbing Felix's arm. The sound came again, clearer this time. In the shallow water near the rocks, something gleamed. Not the mysterious glow they'd seen before, but a physical presence. As their eyes adjusted, they could make out the fish. Its scales were pure gold but dulled by a thick, black coating."It's hurt," Felix said, taking a cautious step forward. The creature's large eyes, fixed upon him. Instead of fear, Felix felt an overwhelming sense of sadness wash over him. Joanna was already rolling up her sleeves. "We need to help it. Look – the oil is all over its gills."They worked quickly and quietly, guided by instinct and their experience helping their father clean fish. But this was different. This fish was alive, and its scales seemed to pulse with an inner light. Joanna ran to gather seaweed and soft kelp while Felix used his shirt to wipe away the oil.

The creature remained still, allowing their touch. Its eye never left them as they worked, and occasionally, they felt what seemed like waves of gratitude washing over them."There," Joanna said finally, sitting back on her heels. "I think that's the last of it."The fish's scales began to glow brighter, and suddenly, both children heard a voice – not in their ears, but in their minds. It was like listening to the sea itself speak, ancient and musical. *Thank you, young ones.* Felix and Joanna stared at each other in amazement."You can talk!" Felix exclaimed in a whisper. *I am Aurelia, Guardian of these waters. Your kindness tonight may have save*d *more than just me.*"Are you the Golden Guardian from Gramps Pete's stories?" Joanna asked. *I have been known by many names through the ages. But now I am weak, and these waters are in grave danger.* "We've noticed," Felix said. "The fish are disappearing, and there's oil everywhere. Can you tell us what's happening?"

Aurelia's glow flickered.*The truth is dark, young ones, and the danger is greater than you know.*

The great fish shifted in the water, and they could see how even that small movement seemed to cost it energy. *I must rest and heal. Will you return tomorrow night?* "Of course we will!" both children said in unison. *Then I will tell you what darkness lurks beneath these waters. But beware – you must tell no one of me.*

Some would do anything to capture a golden fish. "We promise," Felix said solemnly, and Joanna nodded. Aurelia's form began to fade into deeper water. *Until tomorrow then, brave children. And thank you... for remembering how to care.*

They watched the golden fish disappear beneath the waves. They had found the Golden Guardian, but instead of solving their problems, they had stumbled upon an even greater mystery."What do you think is going on?" Joanna asked as they made their way home through the moonlight. Felix shook his head. "I don't know. But whatever it is, we have to help Aurelia fix it."They snuck back into their rooms just as the first hint of dawn touched the horizon. Both children lay awake in their beds, their hands still tingling from touching the golden scales, their minds full of questions about what darkness could be so terrible that it would wound the Golden Guardian, the very protector of all ocean life that Gramps Pete had told them about.

Chapter 5

A Secret Mission

The next day felt endless. Felix could barely focus during breakfast, earning concerned looks from his mother when he poured orange juice into his cereal. Joanna wasn't doing much better, jumping every time someone mentioned fish or the sea."Are you two feeling alright?" their father asked, studying their faces. "You look tired." We're fine!" they answered quickly, in perfect unison. After breakfast, they slipped away to their secret spot behind the lighthouse where they could talk privately."We need a better place to meet Aurelia," Joanna whispered. "Somewhere safer than the open beach."Felix nodded. "Remember that hidden cove past the rocky point? The one where we found all those shells last summer?"

The cove was perfect – sheltered by high rocks on three sides and too difficult for fishing boats to access. They spent the afternoon clearing debris and creating a small channel through the rocks so Aurelia could swim in more easily. That night, they found the Golden Guardian waiting for them in the shallows, her scales already gleaming brighter than before.

Thank you for returning, Aurelia's voice flowed into their minds. The oil you cleaned has allowed me to begin healing."We made you a safe place," Felix said proudly, leading the way to their prepared cove. Aurelia followed, gliding gracefully through the channel they'd cleared. *This is perfect, little ones. Now we can speak freely of what threatens our waters.* The children sat on a smooth rock as Aurelia's expression grew grave. *I have guarded these seas for centuries, but never have I faced a danger like this. They dump their poisons into the sea, thinking no one will notice.*"Is that what's making the fish disappear?" Joanna asked. *Yes. But worse, it's destroying the ancient magic that helps keep our oceans alive. That's why I was too weak to stop them – their poisons affect me more than ordinary creatures.*"But how can we help?" Felix asked. "We're just kids."Aurelia's scales pulsed with a gentle light. *Sometimes the smallest fish swim deepest. I've been watching you both – your kind hearts, your courage. Would you be willing to help me save our waters?* The children nodded without hesitation. *Then I shall grant you a gift.* Aurelia rose slightly in the water, her scales blazing like captured sunlight. *Within you lies the spirit of the sea. I will awaken it.*

Golden light swirled around Felix and Joanna. They felt a tingling sensation in their throats and lungs. *You now can breathe beneath the waves,* Aurelia explained. *But use this gift wisely – it will only last while you're doing the ocean's work.* Felix and Joanna looked at each other in amazement. This was bigger than anything they'd imagined when they'd first heard Gramps Pete's story. *Tomorrow night, we begin,* Aurelia said. *You must find evidence of what they're doing. But remember – tell no one. If the wrong people learn about me...*"We won't let you down," Joanna promised."We'll protect you, and the ocean," Felix added. As they walked home under the stars, they felt different – not just because of Aurelia's gift, but because they now carried a purpose bigger than themselves. Tomorrow their real adventure would begin, deep beneath the waves of Coral Cove.

Chapter 6

Beneath the Waves

The next night was cloudy, perfect for sneaking out unnoticed. Felix and Joanna came to the hidden cove where Aurelia's golden scales provided the only light in the darkness. *Are you ready?* Aurelia asked as they stood at the water's edge."What if it doesn't work?" Joanna whispered, eyeing the dark water nervously. *Trust in the gift,* Aurelia assured them. *The ocean knows its friends.*

Felix took his sister's hand and stepped into the cool water together. At first, it felt like any other swim. Then, as a wave washed over their heads, something magical happened. Instead of holding their breath, they found themselves breathing normally. The water felt as natural as air in their lungs. *Open your eyes,* Aurelia told them. When they did, they gasped in wonder. The underwater world was nothing like they'd imagined. Bioluminescent plankton drifted around them like tiny stars. Schools of silverfish darted past, their scales catching the light from Aurelia's glow. Forests of kelp swayed in the gentle current, creating shadowy gardens that stretched toward the surface.

This is the true heart of the ocean, Aurelia said, as they went deeper. *See how everything is connected?* They watched as tiny fish cleaned larger ones and crabs worked to keep the seafloor tidy. Sea anemones provided homes for little clownfish.

It was like a beautiful underwater city, where every creature had its place. But then Aurelia led them around a coral reef, and the scene changed dramatically. The water was murky and the vibrant colors they'd seen before were muted and grey. Dead coral littered the seafloor like broken bones.

"What happened here?" Felix asked, surprised to find he could speak underwater as easily as on land. *Watch,* Aurelia responded, directing their attention to a dark current that snaked through the water like an evil ribbon. It was the same oily substance they'd found on the beach, now they could see its source. Following the current deeper, they came to an area where the seafloor dropped away sharply. Half-hidden in the gloom, they saw metal pipes emerging from the rock face, spewing dark pollutants into the water. Joanna swam closer to examine the pipes, her hair floating around her like seaweed. "Look at this symbol," she called to Felix, pointing to a metal plate bolted to the rock.

Before he could swim over, a deep rumbling sound filled the water. The pipes shuddered, and a fresh surge of dark liquid burst forth. The current around them suddenly grew stronger. Quick! Aurelia's voice was urgent in their minds. *We must go*! As they hurried back toward the surface, Felix and Joanna couldn't forget what they'd seen. The beauty of the ocean's true nature made the destruction they'd witnessed even more horrifying. But they had found something important – that symbol on the pipes might be the clue they needed. They broke the surface in their hidden cove, breathing normally once again. The transition felt strange after their underwater adventure.

"Did you recognise the symbol?" Felix asked his sister as they caught their breath. Joanna nodded slowly. "I may have seen it on some of the trucks that drive through town to the old industrial park."*Tomorrow, we must learn more,* Aurelia said. *But you've done well. Now you understand what we're fighting for.* As they walked home, their clothes mysteriously dry thanks to Aurelia's magic, Felix and Joanna knew they could never look at the ocean the same way again. Somewhere above them, past the clouds, the moon continued its journey across the sky.

Chapter 7

The Skeptic

Marco Santos had always been observant. As the harbour master's sixteen-year-old son, he'd grown up watching the comings and goings of boats, learning to spot anything unusual in their small fishing community. Lately, something about Felix and Joanna had caught his attention."They're up to something," he muttered to himself, watching the siblings hurry past the harbour office with their father's old camera. They'd been acting strange lately – whispering together, sneaking around the beach, looking guilty whenever anyone approached them. Earlier that morning, he'd overheard them talking behind the fish market."We need proof," Joanna had whispered. "Photos of the pipes, water samples, anything!"But how do we explain how we got them?" Felix had replied. Marco's curiosity was piqued.

That afternoon, as Felix and Joanna made their way toward the rocky point, Marco followed them. He kept his distance, ducking behind boats and rocks whenever they looked back.

The siblings were nervous about something. They stopped at several spots along the beach, taking photos of oil slicks and collecting water samples in small jars. Marco had to admit – something strange was happening to their waters. The fishing had been terrible lately, and he'd seen the unusual dark patches in the water himself. But it was their behaviour at sunset that got his attention.

Instead of heading home, Felix and Joanna toward a hidden cove past the rocky point. Marco knew that area well – it was dangerous to access by boat and was rarely visited. He crept closer, careful to stay hidden behind the rocks. The siblings were sitting on the beach and looking eagerly at the river. Suddenly, a golden glow illuminated the water near them. Marco's jaw dropped. What was that light? He leaned forward, trying to get a better look, but his foot dislodged a loose stone. It clattered down the rocks, sending a sharp echo through the cove.

The siblings were nervous about something. They stopped at several spots along the beach, taking photos of oil slicks and collecting water samples in small jars. Marco had to admit – something strange was happening to their waters. The fishing had been terrible lately, and he'd seen the unusual dark patches in the water himself. But it was their behaviour at sunset that got his attention. Instead of heading home, Felix and Joanna toward a hidden cove past the rocky point. Marco knew that area well – it was dangerous to access by boat and was rarely visited. He crept closer, careful to stay hidden behind the rocks. The siblings were sitting on the beach and looking eagerly at the river. Suddenly, a golden glow illuminated the water near them. Marco's jaw dropped. What was that light? He leaned forward, trying to get a better look, but his foot dislodged a loose stone. It clattered down the rocks, sending a sharp echo through the cove. Felix and Joanna jumped up in alarm. The golden glow instantly vanished."Who's there?" Felix called out, his voice shaking slightly. Marco pressed himself against the rocks, hardly daring to breathe. After a tense moment, he heard the siblings whispering urgently."Do you think someone saw it?

Felix and Joanna jumped up in alarm. The golden glow instantly vanished."Who's there?" Felix called out, his voice shaking slightly. Marco pressed himself against the rocks, hardly daring to breathe. After a tense moment, he heard the siblings whispering urgently."Do you think someone saw it? "We need to go – now!"But what about..."Tomorrow. It's not safe tonight."He waited until their footsteps faded before emerging from his hiding place. The water was dark now, showing no sign of the mysterious light he'd seen. But something caught his eye on the sand – one of their sample jars had fallen from their backpack in their hurry to leave. Marco picked it up, examining the dark water inside. This wasn't just normal ocean water. There was something else in it, something that shouldn't be there. The next morning, he was waiting for them outside their house."Going somewhere?" he asked, holding up the sample jar. Felix and Joanna froze on their front steps, exchanging panicked looks."I saw you last night," Marco continued, his voice low. "The hidden cove, the golden light in the water. What exactly are you two up to?"We... we don't know what you're talking about," Joanna stammered."Really?" Marco raised an eyebrow.

"Then you won't mind if I show this water sample to my father? Or tell him about the strange lights I saw?"Wait!" Felix stepped forward, glancing nervously at his sister. "We can explain."I'm listening," Marco said, crossing his arms. The siblings shared another look, having a silent conversation with their eyes. Finally, Joanna spoke."Not here," she said quietly. "Meet us at the cove tonight at sunset. We'll show you everything."But if you tell anyone before then," Felix added, trying to sound braver than he felt, "you'll ruin our only chance to save the ocean."Marco studied their faces for a long moment. These weren't the looks of kids playing a game or causing trouble. Whatever was going on had to be serious."Sunset then," he agreed, handing back the jar. "But this better be good."As he walked away, Felix and Joanna could only hope they were making the right decision. How would Aurelia react to their secret being discovered? And could they trust Marco with the truth about the Golden Guardian?

Chapter 8

Unlikely Allies

Felix and Joanna waited nervously by their usual spot at the riverbank. They had agreed to show Marco their secret. They spotted him walking towards them, his face full of curiosity, Joanna squeezed Felix's hand."Okay, you said you'd explain everything," Marco said, looking around expectantly. "What's so special about this part of the river?"Sometimes secrets must be shared with those who can help, Aurelia's gentle voice touched their thoughts.

Marco jumped. "What was that? I just heard... in my head..."A golden gleam rippled through the water, and Aurelia rose to the surface. The morning sunlight danced across her scales, creating tiny rainbows on the water."Oh... my... " Marco stumbled backwards, nearly falling. "Is that... is that a golden fish?"*Yes, young Marco. And I need help from brave friends like you.* Marco sank on a nearby rock, his mouth open. "This is... this is incredible! A fish that can speak in our minds!" His face suddenly lit up. "Wait – is this why the river's water samples have been so strange?"Water samples?" Joanna leaned forward.

"My dad works for environmental protection. He's been worried about this river." Marco's excitement grew. "He says something's polluting it, but they can't figure out what." *The poison comes from upstream,* Aurelia said. *It grows stronger each day.* "The old factory!" Marco jumped up. "Dad mentioned lights there at night, even though it's supposed to be empty." Felix grabbed a stick and drew in the dirt. "Where exactly is this factory?" As Marco pointed out locations on their makeshift map, Joanna took notes in her small notebook. *You must be careful,* Aurelia warned. *Those who are harming the river, will not welcome young heroes.* "We'll be cautious," Marco promised. His earlier scepticism had vanished completely. "I can show you how to collect water samples properly. Dad taught me everything about it." "So you'll help us?" Felix asked. "Try and stop me! This is the most amazing thing that's ever happened!" Marco said excitedly. "A magical fish, evil polluters, a mystery to solve – count me in!"

They spent the next hour planning their investigation of the factory. With Marco's knowledge of environmental testing and his father's work, they finally had a real chance to save the river. The sun climbed higher as they finished their plans. Tomorrow they would begin their mission properly – no longer just kids with a magical fish friend, but three determined allies with a purpose. *Goodbye,* Aurelia whispered in their minds as she slipped beneath the surface. *Thank you, Marco, for joining our cause.* Marco watched the golden ripples fade with wonder in his eyes. "Same time tomorrow?"Felix and Joanna nodded. Their secret circle had grown by one, but somehow, it felt exactly right.

Chapter 9

Race Against Time

"Look at these," Marco whispered, pulling some papers from his backpack. "I borrowed these from Dad's office. The factory has a schedule for waste disposal. A big one's planned for tomorrow night."Joanna's hands trembled as she read the document. "That's... that's thousands of gallons!"We have to tell someone," Felix insisted. "Your dad, Marco – he'd believe us, right?"Marco shook his head grimly. "I tried. He just patted my head and said I must have misread the papers. Nobody believes kids."They hurried back to their meeting spot by the river. The water looked murkier than usual and Aurelia took longer to appear. *Something is wrong. The water... it burns.* Aurelia said, her voice faint. The children gasped. Aurelia's usually brilliant golden scales had dulled, and she moved sluggishly through the water. "They're planning to dump more waste tomorrow night", Joanna said. *Then we have little time,* Aurelia's voice wavered. *The river cannot survive such poison.*

"I tried telling my science teacher," Felix said desperately. She said I had an 'active imagination' and should write stories instead. Marco paced along the riverbank. We could call the newspaper," he said. They'd never believe us either," Felix sighed. We're just kids."*But you are not just children,* Aurelia's voice, though weak, carried a spark of determination. *You are my friends, and you can see what others cannot.*

Suddenly, Marco snapped his fingers. "The evidence! Dad always says you need evidence. I know how to use his water testing kit and camera."But we'd need to catch them in the act," Joanna said."Then that's what we'll do," Felix stood up straighter. "Tomorrow night, we'll document everything.*"Be careful, my friends,* Aurelia warned. *The darkness hides many dangers.*"We have to try," Joanna said firmly, watching Aurelia struggle to stay upright in the water.

"No one else will help."They spent the next hour planning their mission. Marco would bring his dad's camera and water testing kit. Joanna and Felix who lived closest to the factory, would keep watch during the day and inform Marco if they saw any movement. Felix would bring his fathers's night vision monocular that he'd gotten for his birthday."We'll meet here at sunset," Marco said, checking his map one last time. "That gives us time to get into position before dark."*I wish I could help more,* Aurelia's voice was barely a whisper now. *But the poison... it weakens me.*"Save your strength, Aurelia," Joanna knelt by the water's edge. "We'll handle this."As they watched, Aurelia disappeared beneath the murky surface, her golden glow now barely visible. They had less than thirty-six hours to save their friend and the river."What if we fail?" Felix voiced the fear they all shared."We won't," Marco said firmly. "We can't."Joanna nodded, her jaw set with determination. "Tomorrow night, we stop them. No matter what."As they walked home, each lost in their thoughts, they knew their biggest challenge lay ahead. They might be just kids and the river's last hope. Sometimes, the most unlikely heroes are the ones who make the biggest difference.

Chapter 10

The Daring Plan

Sunset painted the sky orange as three shadows crept through the undergrowth near the old factory. Marco clutched his father's camera, Felix adjusted the night vision monocular, and Joanna checked her phone's signal."Look," Felix whispered, pointing. "That truck's got the 'Chemical Disposal' logo – just like the one Dad showed us in the photos."Marco nodded grimly. "They're bringing in waste from other factories too. That's why they only dump at night."*Be careful, my friends,* Aurelia's weak voice touched their minds. *The men are inside. I sense their movements.* They had positioned themselves around the factory's rear entrance. Marco hid behind a large oak tree with the best view of the pipes. Joanna crouched where she could see men unloading large drums from the truck. Felix stayed closest to the river, preparing to take samples. The factory door creaked open. Two men emerged, speaking in low voices."Get those drums inside," one said. "Midnight's the best time to dump it all."

" The Boss wants everything gone by morning," the other replied, rolling a barrel down the truck's ramp. "Can't risk another inspection."Joanna's phone buzzed silently in their group chat: "Got photos of truck and license plate. They're mixing something with the factory waste."Marco steadied his camera. The security lights cast long shadows across the factory yard, creating perfect hiding spots. But they also made photography tricky – too much flash would give them away. Felix's legs had gone numb from crouching when he heard the rumble of machinery starting up.

They begin, Aurelia warned. The children watched in horror as something began to flow through the pipes and into the river. It was thick, dark, and smelled terrible. Marco started filming.

His hands shook, but he forced himself to hold steady. Evidence. They needed evidence. Felix carefully filled the sample bottles, marking each one with the time and date as Marco had shown him. The liquid looked even worse up close – oily rainbows swirling on its surface. Joanna's urgent message lit up their phones: "Someone is coming!" *The poison spread too quickly,* Aurelia's voice was barely a whisper now. *I will try to help.* They felt Aurelia gathering her remaining power. Then the river started to flow peculiarly, moving backwards near the pipe's outlet and forming a small whirlpool that trapped most of the pollution. That's when the floodlights blazed on. "Hey! What's going on down there?" a voice called out. Through the glare, they saw a man in a business suit standing at the factory door, flanked by the workers. "Just some kids, Mr. Reynolds," one worker said, shining his flashlight toward them. The factory owner's face darkened as he spotted Marco's camera. "What do you think you're doing here? This is private property!" Felix clutched the water samples. Joanna's phone was still recording. Marco's camera captured everything. *Now is the time,* Aurelia's voice, though weak, was determined. *Show them what you have found.*

Marco stepped forward, surprising everyone including himself. His voice shook but grew stronger as he spoke. "We know what you're doing to the river. We have proof. And if anything happens to us, it's already been sent to people who can help."This wasn't entirely true – they hadn't sent anything yet. But Mr. Reynolds didn't know that. The factory owner's face shifted from anger to worry. Behind him, the truck's driver was slowly backing away. Listen, kids," Mr. Reynolds said, his voice suddenly nervous, "surely we can talk about this..."But the children were already backing toward the river path, clutching their evidence. They had what they needed. Now they just had to get it to someone who would listen - if they could get away. The owner took another step forward, his face hardening. "Hand over those cameras, now."*My friends,* Aurelia's voice came suddenly stronger in their minds. *Brace yourselves.* With the last of her strength, Aurelia summoned a massive wave that rose from the river like a liquid wall. The children watched in awe as the water crashed over the factory yard, sending Mr. Reynolds and his workers sprawling.

"Run!" Felix yelled, already turning. The three children sprinted down the river path, their precious evidence clutched tight, while behind them the factory owner and his workers were still trying to get to their feet in the muddy puddles. *Go... quickly...* Aurelia's voice was barely a whisper now, exhausted from the effort. They ran until they couldn't hear the angry shouts anymore, their hearts pounding, their clothes splashed with river water. But they were safe. And more importantly, they had their proof.

Chapter 11

A Sea Change

The morning sun streamed through the town hall windows, filling every seat. Marco's father, Mr Enzo from the Environmental Protection Agency, stood at the podium, his face grave as he clicked through the photos on the large screen."These images show clear evidence of illegal chemical dumping," he said, glancing at Marco with a mixture of pride and concern. "Along with these certified water samples, we have video documentation of multiple violations."In the front row, Felix, Joanna, and Marco sat together, still hardly believing how quickly everything had happened after they'd shown Marco's dad their evidence the previous morning. The factory owner, Mr. Reynolds, sat across the aisle with his lawyers, his face pale."The chemicals found in these samples," Mr. Enzo continued, "match those from other illegal dumping sites across the state. This wasn't just one factory's waste – they were disposing of hazardous materials from multiple facilities."A murmur of anger rippled through the crowd.

The mayor leaned forward in her chair, her expression thunderous."Immediate cleanup operations will begin today," the mayor announced after Mr. Enzo finished. "I'm calling for community volunteers to help with the river restoration project."Hands shot up across the room. The local fishing club, the high school environmental team, and dozens of concerned citizens volunteered.

Even Mr. Garcia, who owned the garden centre, offered to donate supplies and equipment. The river sings with hope, and Aurelia's voice whispers in the children's minds. Over the next few weeks, the transformation was remarkable. Teams of volunteers worked tirelessly along the riverbanks.

Special equipment filtered the water, while environmental experts monitored the river's recovery. The factory stood silent, its gates padlocked, and "CLOSED BY EPA ORDER" signs were posted everywhere. One sunny afternoon, the three children left the cleanup activities to visit their special spot by the river. The water ran clearer now, sparkling in the sunlight. Aurelia rose to meet them, her scales gleaming with their old brilliance. *Look how the river heals,* she said, her voice strong and clear once more. *Three brave children dared to make a difference.*"We couldn't have done it without you," Joanna said, smiling at the golden fish. "That wave was amazing!"*I could not have survived without you,* Aurelia replied. *The river is my home, but you are my family too*". Will you stay?" Felix asked. "Now that the river's getting better?" *Yes,* Aurelia's voice held a smile. *I will watch over the river and remind those who come after you that even the smallest among us can create great change.* Marco grinned. "Dad says they will turn the factory site into an environmental education centre.

They want to teach kids about protecting rivers and oceans."And we'll be the first volunteers," Joanna enthusiastically added. The children sat by the riverbank, watching volunteers work further downstream. Someone had hung a banner between two trees: "Our River, Our Future." Below it, families worked together, picking up trash, planting riverside flowers, and learning about water protection."You know what?" Felix said thoughtfully. "Maybe that's the real magic. Not just having a talking fish for a friend – though that's pretty amazing – but discovering that we could make things better."*That is the greatest magic of all,* Aurelia agreed. *The power to change the world, one small action at a time.* As the afternoon sun painted the river in gold, the three children and their magical friend watched the water flow past. The river had changed them, just as they had changed the river. And somewhere downstream, perhaps other children would look into the water, see a flash of gold, and realise they had the power to make a difference.

On nights when the moon is full and the tide is high, if you listen carefully, you might hear Aurelia's voice on the wind, reminding you that even the smallest ripple can change the course of a river.